Humphrey's

Corner

To Georgie, Ralph and Kim,
love Mummy x

Henry Holt and Company, LLC
Publishers since 1866
115 West 18th Street
New York, New York 10011
www.henryholt.com

Library of Congress Cataloging-in-Publication Data
Hunter, Sally.
Humphrey's corner / Sally Hunter.
Summary: A little elephant tries out different spots around the house.
until he finds the perfect place to play—near his mother.
(1. Elephants—Fiction. 2. Mother and child—Fiction.) I. Title.
PZ7.H9183 Hu 2001 (E)—dc21 00-47135

ISBN 0-8050-6786-8 (hardcover)
5 7 9 11 13 15 14 12 10 8 6
ISBN 0-8050-7397-3 (paperback)
1 3 5 7 9 10 8 6 4 2

First published in hardcover in 2001 by Henry Holt and Company
First Owlet paperback edition—2003
Printed in Singapore

Humphrey's Corner

Sally Hunter

Henry Holt and Company

New York

Humphrey was looking
for his rabbit, Mop.
He wanted to go and play
but he had to have Mop,
otherwise it just wasn't right.

Humphrey found Mop and
his blanket, Mooey,
squashed beside
the bed.

He thought the
stool might be good
to play with, too.

So Humphrey put
his Mooey
and the little stool
into a box
with Mop on top
(so he could see where he was going) . . .

Humphrey

and went to find somewhere interesting to play.

He found some pretty colors . . .

. . . sploshy sounds . . .

and a house for Mop.

Mop was sick and needed his medicine . . .

but the floor was a bit hard
and there was sticky stuff
everywhere.

It wasn't quite right.

So Humphrey put
his Mooey,
the little stool,
and the bottle with pretty colors
into the box
with Mop on top . . .

and walked away to look for somewhere cozy to play.

Humphrey peeped in.
It was all pink and sunny . . .

. . . and smelled just like Mommy . . .

. . . with lots of

very pretty things

to look at.

Mop was in a boat sailing
in a sparkly blue sea . . .

but it was a bit dark
and quiet.

It wasn't quite right.

So Humphrey put
his Mooey,
the little stool,
the bottle with the pretty colors, and
Mommy's sparkly necklace into the box
with Mop on top . . .

and walked away to look for somewhere
different to play.

He found a very nice hidey-hole.

Mop needed
his afternoon nap . . .

but there were lots of
gurgly, clanky noises.

Mop said he was too hot.

It wasn't quite right.

So Humphrey put
his Mooey,
the little stool,
the bottle with the pretty colors,
Mommy's sparkly necklace,
and his favorite towel with the ducks on it
into the box
with Mop on top . . .

and walked away to look for somewhere else
to play.

Humphrey had a
bit of a problem
with the stairs . . .

and his box . . .

. . . and because Mop was on the top he fell,

flop,

plop,

down the stairs.

Humphrey wanted to fetch
Mop, but he couldn't leave his box in
case that fell, too.

He suddenly felt tired
and didn't want to play anymore.

"Are you all right, little love?" asked Mommy.

Mommy picked up the box, gave Mop back to Humphrey, and helped them both downstairs.

Humphrey followed Mommy into the kitchen.
It was snug and warm . . .

...with nice treats on the table...

. . . and a very special place.

It was Humphrey's and Mop's
secret castle.
Mop was a king on his throne,
with jewels and treasure.

It was very cozy . . .

. . . and near Mommy.

It was just right.